Aesop's Fables

ILLUSTRATED BY

Pat Stewart

DOVER PUBLICATIONS, INC.
New York

DOVER CHILDREN'S THRIFT CLASSICS
EDITOR OF THIS VOLUME: CANDACE WARD

Bibliographical Note

Aesop's Fables is a new selection of fables traditionally attributed to Aesop. The text has been adapted from *Aesop's Fables*, Cassell & Company, Limited, London, n.d., and other standard editions. The illustrations and the note have been specially prepared for this edition.

Library of Congress Cataloging-in-Publication Data

Aesop's fables. English. Selections
    Aesop's fables / illustrated by Pat Stewart.
       p.   cm.—(Dover children's thrift classics)
    Summary: A collection of concise stories told by the Greek slave, Aesop.
   ISBN-13: 978-0-486-28020-2
   ISBN-10: 0-486-28020-9
    1. Fables [1. Fables.] I. Aesop. II. Stewart, Pat Ronson, ill.
III. Title. IV. Series.
PZ8.2.A254Ste 1994
[398.24′52]—dc20
                                            94-8782
                                           CIP
                                           AC

Manufactured in the United States by R R Donnelley
28020917   2016
www.doverpublications.com

Note

The name Aesop has been associated with the fable for at least 2,000 years. Even though it is uncertain whether such a person even existed, he has traditionally been hailed as the creator of the genre. While this claim has been contradicted by historical and scholarly research, popular tradition attributes most fables, regardless of their origins, to Aesop.

The story of Aesop's life has often taken on the same legendary proportions as his literary reputation. According to Herodotus, the fifth-century Greek historian, Aesop—the "maker of stories"—lived in the mid-sixth century. Herodotus also tells us that Aesop was a slave, and that he was killed by the people of Delphi, perhaps for seditious or sacrilegious beliefs. From these bare facts, Aesop's legend grew, and by the time that Sir Roger L'Estrange published his collection of *Fables* in 1692, Aesop had acquired the rather grotesque physical appearance that served as a marked contrast to his wit and wisdom. In fact, according to L'Estrange, Aesop, with his flat nose, humped back and misshapen head, was the "most scandalous figure of a man that ever was heard of."

Whatever Aesop's physical appearance, the fables attributed to him have remained popular for centuries. Most of the fables in this edition feature the animals that seem so human in their wit, vanity and benevolence: the clever Fox, the presumptuous Ass and the valiant Mouse. The morals, too, have become as familiar as the animals, and they hold as much wisdom today as ever.

Contents

Contents

Contents

Contents

Aesop's Fables

The Ants and the Grasshopper

A Grasshopper that had merrily sung all summer long, was almost perishing with hunger in the winter. So she went to some Ants that lived nearby, and asked them to lend her a little of the food they had stored. "You shall certainly be paid before this time of year comes again," she said. "What did you do all the summer?" they asked. "Why, all day long, and all night long too, I sang, if you please," answered the Grasshopper. "Oh, you sang, did you?" said the Ants. "Well, now you can dance too."

MORAL: Don't neglect the future in times of plenty, for tomorrow you may need what you wasted today.

The Wolf in Sheep's Clothing

A Wolf, wrapping himself in the skin of a Sheep, was able to sneak into a sheepfold, where he devoured several young Lambs. The Shepherd, however, soon discovered him and killed him and hung him up to a tree, still in his disguise. Some other Shepherds passing that way, thought it was a Sheep hanging there, and cried to their friend, "Is that the way you treat Sheep in this part of the country?" "No, friends," he cried swinging the carcass around so that they might see what it was, "but it is the way to treat Wolves, even if they are dressed in Sheep's clothing."

MORAL: A person's true nature will reveal itself despite disguise.

The Jackdaw and the Pigeons

A Jackdaw, seeing how well some Pigeons in a certain dovecote ate, and how happily they lived together, wished very much to join them. So, he whitened his feathers and slipped in among the Pigeons one evening just as it was getting dark. As long as he kept quiet he escaped notice, but soon he grew bolder, and feeling very jolly in his new home, he burst into a hearty laugh. His voice betrayed him. The Pigeons set upon him and drove him out. Afterwards when he tried to join the Jackdaws again, his discolored and battered feathers drew their attention to him. When his old friends found out what he had been up to, they would have nothing more to do with him.

MORAL: Be true to yourself, or run the risk of losing the respect of others.

The Belly and the Members

In olden days, when all a man's limbs did not work together as peacefully as they do now, but when each had a will and way of its own, the Members began to criticize the Belly for enjoying a life of idleness and luxury, while they spent all their time working to feed it. So they entered into a conspiracy to cut off the Belly's supplies in the future. The Hands were no longer to carry food to the Mouth, nor would the Mouth receive the food, nor the Teeth chew it. They had not long followed this plan of starving the Belly, when they all began, one by one, to fail and flag, and the whole body began to pine away. Then the Members realized that the Belly, too, cumbersome and useless as it seemed, had an important function of its own; that they could no more do without it than it could do without them; and that if they wanted to keep the body in a healthy state, they must work together, each in his proper sphere, for the common good of all.

MORAL: Only by working together can the greatest good for all be achieved.

The Lion and the Four Bulls

Four Bulls were such great friends that they always ate together. A Lion watched them for many days with longing eyes, but since they were never far apart from each other, he was afraid to attack them. At length he succeeded in making them jealous of one another, and their jealousy eventually turned into a mutual aversion. When they strayed far away from each other, the Lion fell upon them singly, and killed them all.

MORAL: The quarrels of friends are the opportunities of enemies.

The Goatherd and the She-Goat

One evening, a Boy, whose job it was to look after some Goats, gathered them together to lead them home. One of them, a She-Goat, refused to obey his call, and stood on a ledge of a rock, nibbling the grass that grew there. The Boy lost all patience, and picking up a great stone, threw it at the Goat with all his might. The stone struck one of the Goat's horns and broke it off at the middle. The Boy, terrified at what he had done and afraid of his master's anger, threw himself on his knees before the Goat and begged her to say nothing about the accident, swearing that he never meant to aim the stone so well. "Tush!" replied the Goat. "Even if I say nothing at all, my horn is sure to tell the tale."

MORAL: Facts speak plainer than words.

The Fox and the Stork

One day a Fox invited a Stork to dine with him, and, deciding to play a joke on the Stork, he put the soup that he had for dinner in a large flat dish. Although the Fox himself could lap it up quite well, the Stork could only dip in the tips of his long bill. Some time after, the Stork, remembering the Fox's trick, invited him to dinner. He, in his turn, put some minced meat in a long, narrow-necked jar, into which he could easily put his bill, while the Fox was forced to be content licking what ran down the sides of the jar. The Fox then remembered his old trick, and had to admit that the Stork had paid him back in his own coin.

MORAL: Don't complain when others treat you as you treat them.

The Town Mouse and the Country Mouse

A Country Mouse, a plain, sensible sort of fellow, was once visited by a former companion of his, who had moved to a neighboring city. The Country Mouse put before his friend some fine peas, some choice bacon, and a bit of rare old Stilton cheese, and told him to enjoy his dinner. The City Mouse nibbled a little here and there in a dainty manner, wondering at the pleasure his host took in such plain and ordinary food. After dinner, the Town Mouse said to the Country Mouse, "Really, my good friend, how can

you be happy in this dismal, boring place? You go on and on, in a dull humdrum sort of way, from one year's end to another. Come with me, this very night, and see with your own eyes what a life I lead." The Country Mouse agreed, and as soon as it was dark, off they started for the city, where they arrived just as a splendid supper given by the master of the house where our town friend lived was over. The City Mouse soon got together a heap of dainties on a corner of the handsome Turkish carpet. The Country Mouse, who had never even heard the names of half the meats set before him, was wondering where to begin, when the door creaked, opened, and in came a servant with a light. The companions ran off, but as soon as it was quiet again, they returned to their dinner. Once more the door opened, and the son of the master of the house came in with a great bounce, followed by his little dog, who ran sniffing to the very spot where our friends had just been. The City Mouse was by that time safe in his hole—which, by the way, he had not been thoughtful enough to show to his friend, who had to hide behind a sofa, where he waited in fear and trembling until it was quiet again. The City Mouse then called upon him to finish his supper, but the Country Mouse said, "No, no; I'm leaving as fast as I can. I would rather have a crust of bread with peace and quiet than all your fine things in the middle of such alarms and frights as these."

MORAL: A simple life without worries is better than a rich life full of cares.

The Cock and the Jewel

As a Cock was scratching up the straw in a farmyard in search of food, he found a beautiful Jewel. "Ho!" he said, "you are a very fine thing, I'm sure, to those who prize you; but give me a barley-corn before all the pearls in the world."

MORAL: Beauty without usefulness is sometimes undesirable.

The Serpent and the Man

A Child was playing in a field at the back of his Father's house, when accidentally he stepped on a Snake, which turned round and bit him. The Child died of the bite, and the Father, chasing the Snake, tried to kill him with an axe, but only succeeded in cutting off a piece of his tail. The Snake reached his hole, and the next day the Man came back and laid some honey, meal, and salt outside the hole, and offered to make up, thinking to entice the Snake out and kill him. "It won't do," hissed out the Snake. "As long as I miss my tail, and you your Child, there can be no goodwill between us."

MORAL: A serious quarrel is not easily made up.

The Travelers and the Plane Tree

Some Travelers, one hot summer day, saw a Plane tree nearby and made straight for it. Throwing themselves on the ground, they rested under its shade. As they lay looking up toward the tree, they said to each other, "What

a useless tree is this fruitless Plane!" But the Plane tree answered them, "Ungrateful creatures! At the very moment you are enjoying my shade, you criticize me for being good-for-nothing."

MORAL: Ingratitude is as blind as it is base.

The Eagle and the Arrow

A Bowman took aim at an Eagle and hit him in the heart. As the Eagle turned his head in the agonies of death, he noticed that the Arrow was winged with his own feathers. "How much sharper," he said, "are the wounds made by weapons that we ourselves have supplied!"

MORAL: We often supply the means for our own destruction.

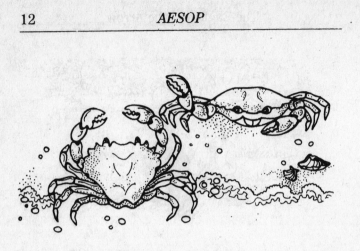

The Two Crabs

"My dear," called out an old Crab to her daughter one day, "why do you sidle along in that awkward manner? Why don't you walk straight like other people?" "Well, mother," answered the young Crab, "it seems to me that I walk exactly like you do. Go first and show me how, and I will gladly follow."

MORAL: It is better to teach by example than by words alone.

The Fox and the Woodman

A Fox being chased by some Hunters came up to a man who was cutting wood, and begged him for a place to hide. The man showed him his own hut, and the Fox crept in and hid himself in a corner. The Hunters presently came up and asked the man whether he had seen the Fox. "No," he replied, but at the same time, he pointed his finger to the corner. They, however, did not understand the hint and were off again immediately. When the Fox perceived that they were out of sight, he was stealing off without saying a word. But the man stopped him, saying, "Is this the way you leave your host, without a word of thanks for your safety?" "A pretty host!" said the Fox, turning round upon him. "If you had been as honest with your fingers as you were with your tongue, I would not have left without saying goodbye."

MORAL: Actions speak louder than words.

The Lark and Her Young Ones

A Lark, who had Young Ones in a field of corn that was almost ripe, was afraid that the reapers would come before her young brood were able to fly. So every day when she flew away to look for food, she told them to remember what they heard in her absence, and to tell her about it when she returned. One day when she was gone, they heard the Farmer say to his son that the corn seemed ripe enough to be cut. He then told him to go early the next day and ask their friends and neighbors to come and help to reap it. When the old Lark came home, the Little Ones, quivering and chirping all around her, told her what had happened and begged her to move them as fast as she could. But the mother reassured them, "for," she said, "if the Farmer depends on his friends and his neighbors, I am sure the corn will not be reaped tomorrow." The next day she went out again, and left the same orders as before. The Farmer came and waited. The sun grew hot, but nothing was done, for not a soul came to help reap the corn. "You see," he said to his son, "these friends of ours are not to be depended on, so go to your uncles and cousins, and say I wish them to come tomorrow morning and help us to reap." The Young Ones in a great fright, reported this to their mother as soon as she returned. "Do not be frightened, children," she said. "Kindred and relations are not always very quick to help one another; but keep your ears open, and let me know what you hear tomor-

row." The Farmer came the next day, and finding his relations as undependable as his neighbors, said to his son, "Now, George, listen to me. Get a couple of good sickles ready for tomorrow morning, for we must reap the corn by ourselves." The Young Ones told this to their mother. "Then, my dears," she said, "it is time for us to go indeed, for when a man decides to do his work himself, it isn't likely that he will be disappointed." So she removed her Young Ones immediately, and the corn was reaped the next day by the old man and his son.

MORAL: The surest way to get something done is to do it yourself.

The Wolf and the Watchdog

One night, a Wolf, who was so hungry he was almost skin and bone, met a large, sleek Dog, who was as strong as he was fat. The Wolf would gladly have made a meal of him, but he knew he could never win a fight with the Dog in his condition. So, bidding the Dog goodnight very humbly, he praised his good looks. "It would be easy for you," replied the Dog, "to be as fat as I am, if you liked. Leave this forest, where you and your friends can hardly find enough to eat and often die of hunger. Follow me, and you shall live much better." "What do I have to do?" asked the Wolf. "Almost nothing," answered the Dog; "just chase away robbers, and fawn upon the folks of the house. You will, in return, be fed all sorts of nice things—bones and tablescraps—to say nothing of many a friendly pat on the head." The Wolf, at the picture of so much comfort, nearly shed tears of joy. They trotted off together, but, as they went along, the Wolf noticed a bare spot on the Dog's neck. "What is that mark?" he asked. "Oh, nothing," said the Dog, "only the merest trifle. The collar I wear when I am tied up rubs my fur." "Tied up!" exclaimed the Wolf, with a sudden stop. "Tied up! You mean you cannot always run where you please?" "Well, not always," said the Dog. "But what does that matter?" "It matters so much to me," rejoined the Wolf, "that your life shall not be mine at any price!" And leaping away, he ran once more to his native forest.

MORAL: Luxury without freedom is not worth having.

The Dog and His Shadow

A Dog, carrying in his mouth a piece of meat that he had stolen, was crossing a smooth stream over a bridge. Looking down, he saw what he thought was another dog carrying another piece of meat. Snapping greedily to get this as well, he dropped the meat that he had, and lost it in the stream.

MORAL: Be satisfied with what you have.

The Old Man, His Son and the Ass

An Old Man and his little Boy were once driving their Ass to the next market town, where they were going to sell it. "Have you no more sense" said a passerby, "than for you and your Son to trudge on foot, and let your Ass go unburdened?" So the Man put his Boy on the Ass, and they went on again. "You lazy young rascal!" said the next person they met. "Aren't you ashamed to ride while your poor old Father goes on foot?" The Man lifted off the Boy, and got up on the Ass himself. Two women passed by soon after, and one said to the other, "Look at that selfish old fellow, riding while his little Son follows behind on foot!" The Old Man then picked up the Boy and set him behind him. The next traveler they met asked the Old Man whether or not the Ass was his own. When the Man answered that it was, the stranger said, "No one would think so from the way that you treat it. Why, you are better able to carry the poor animal than he is to carry both of you." At that, the Old Man tied the Ass's legs to a long pole, and he and his Son picked it up, staggering along under its weight. In that fashion they entered the town, and their appearance caused so much laughter that the Old Man, mad with vexation at the result of all his efforts to satisfy everybody, threw the Ass into the river and seizing his Son by the arm, went back home again.

MORAL: By trying to please everyone, you please no one, least of all yourself.

The Fox and the Lion

When a Fox, who had never seen a Lion before, met one for the very first time, he was so terrified that he almost died of fright. When he met him the second time, he was still afraid, but managed to disguise his fear. When he saw him the third time, he was so much emboldened that he went up to him and asked him how he did.

MORAL: Familiarity breeds contempt.

The Leopard and the Fox

One day the Fox overheard the Leopard praising his own beautifully spotted coat. The Fox then told him that, handsome as he might be, he considered himself a great deal handsomer. "Your beauty is of the body," said the Fox; "mine is of the mind."

MORAL: Physical beauty is only skin-deep.

Minerva's Olive

Each of the gods used to have a favorite tree. Jupiter preferred the oak, Venus the myrtle, Apollo the laurel, Cybele the pine, and Hercules the poplar. Minerva, surprised that they should choose trees which bore no fruit, asked Jupiter the reason. "It is," he said, "to prevent any one thinking that we only chose the trees for what they could give us." "Let fools think what they please," returned Minerva, "I shall not scruple to acknowledge that I choose the Olive tree for the usefulness of its fruit." "O daughter," replied the father of the gods, "it is with justice that men esteem thee wise, for nothing is truly valuable that is not useful."

MORAL: Utility is often the final measure of worth.

The Countryman and the Snake

A Countryman returning home one winter's day found a Snake by the roadside half dead with cold. Feeling sorry for the creature, he brought it home to his fireside to revive it. No sooner had the warmth restored the Snake than it began to attack the Man's children. Upon this the Countryman, whose compassion had saved its life, took up a stick and laid the Snake dead at his feet.

MORAL: Those who return evil for good should not expect the kindness of others to last long.

The Wolf and the Kid

A Wolf spied a Kid that had strayed from his herd, and pursued him. The Kid, finding that he could not escape, waited until the Wolf came up, and then assuming a cheerful tone, said, "I see clearly enough that I must be eaten, but I prefer to die as pleasantly as I can. Play me, therefore, a few notes on your pipe before I die." The Wolf, who was of a musical turn and always carried his pipe with him, played a tune and the Kid danced. Soon the noise of the pipe brought the Sheepdogs to the spot. The Wolf ran off, saying, "This is what happens when people stray from their profession. My business was to play the butcher, not the piper."

MORAL: Those who stray from their true business often lose the prize in hand.

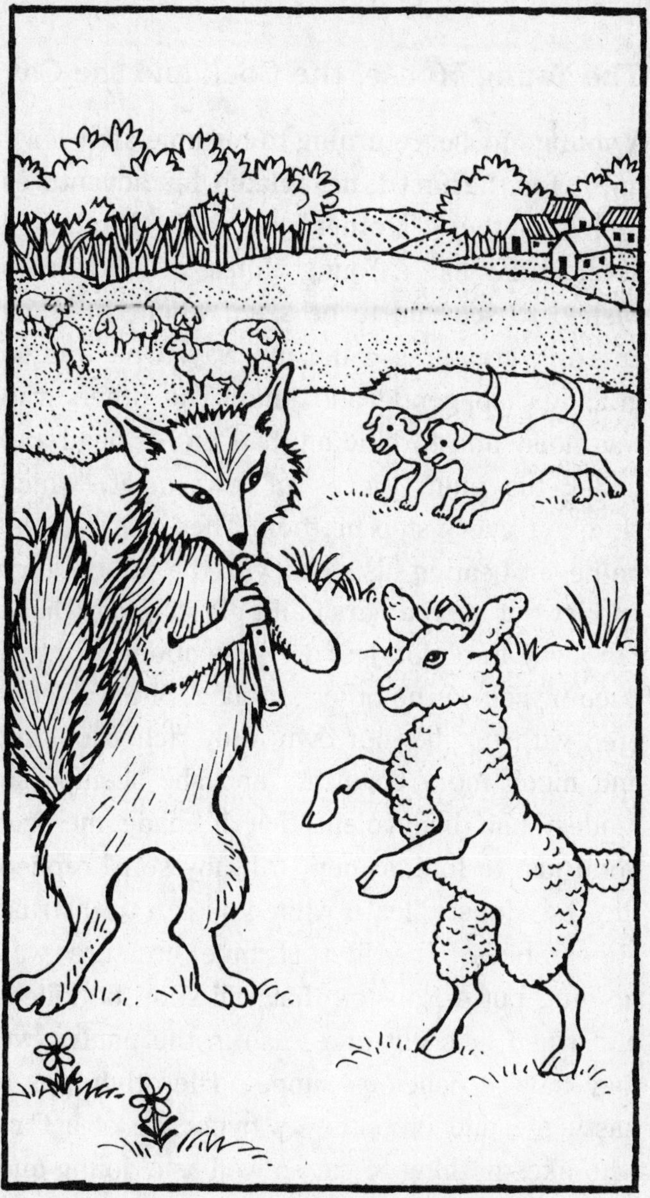

The Young Mouse, the Cock and the Cat

A young Mouse, returning to his hole after leaving it for the first time, related his adventures to his mother: "Mother," he said, "I rambled about today like a Young Mouse of spirit, who wished to see and to be seen, when two such amazing creatures came my way! One was so gracious, so gentle and kind! The other, who was noisy and forbidding, had on his head and under his chin, pieces of raw meat, which shook at every step he took. Then, all at once, he began beating his sides with the utmost fury and let out such a harsh and piercing cry that I ran away in terror, just as I was about to introduce myself to the other stranger. She was covered with fur like our own, only richer-looking and much more beautiful, and she seemed so modest and benevolent that it made me feel good just to look at her." "Ah, my son," replied the Old Mouse, "learn while you can to distrust appearances. The first strange creature was nothing but a Rooster, that will soon be killed, and when he's put on a dish in the pantry, we may have a delicious supper. The other was a nasty, sly, and bloodthirsty hypocrite of a Cat, who likes nothing to eat so well as a young and juicy little Mouse like yourself!"

MORAL: Don't be deceived by grand appearances.

The Vain Jackdaw

A Jackdaw once dressed himself in feathers that had fallen from some Peacocks and strutted about in the company of these birds, trying to pass himself off as one of them. They soon found him out and pulled their feathers from him so roughly and battered him so badly, that when he tried to rejoin the other Jackdaws, they, in their turn, would have nothing to do with him, and drove him from their society.

MORAL: Be content with what nature made you, or run the risk of earning contempt by trying to be what you're not.

Belling the Cat

A certain Cat that lived in a large house was so vigilant and active, that the Mice held a large meeting to consider what to do. Many plans had been presented and dismissed, when a young Mouse, rising and catching the eye of the president, said that he had a proposal to make, which he was sure would meet with the approval of everyone. "If," he said, "the Cat wore a little bell around her neck, every step she took would make it tinkle; then, always warned of her approach, we would have time to reach our holes. This way, we could live in safety, and defy her power." The speaker resumed his seat with a complacent air, and a murmur of applause arose from the audience. An old grey Mouse, with a twinkle in his eye, then got up, and said that the young Mouse's plan was admirable, but that it had one drawback: Who should put the bell around the Cat's neck?

MORAL: It is easier to propose a plan than to put it into action.

The Covetous Man

A Miser once buried all his money in the ground, at the foot of a tree, and went every day to feast upon the sight of his treasure. A thief, who had watched him at this occupation, came one night and carried off the gold. The next day the Miser, finding his treasure gone, tore his clothes and filled the air with his cries. One of his neighbors told him that, since he didn't spend the money anyway, he hadn't really lost anything. "Go every day," he said, "and just pretend your money is there, and you'll be as well off as ever."

MORAL: The value of money is not in having it, but in using it wisely.

The One-Eyed Doe

A Doe that had only one eye, used to graze near the sea, so that she might keep her blind eye toward the water, while she watched the countryside with the other to make sure that no hunters approached from that side. One day, however, some men in a boat saw her, and as she could not see them approach, they were able to come very close to the shore and shoot her. As she was dying, she cried out, "Alas, hard fate! that I should be shot from the side from which I expected no harm and be safe on that where I looked for most danger."

MORAL: Often those things we most feared do us no harm, while the things we believed were harmless prove most dangerous.

The Cock and the Fox

A Cock, perched among the branches of a lofty tree, crowed aloud. The shrillness of his voice echoed through the woods and the well-known sound brought a hungry Fox, who was prowling in search of prey, to the spot. Reynard, as the Fox is called, saw that the Cock was at a great height, and so decided to use his wits to bring him down. He greeted the bird in his mildest voice, and said, "Haven't you heard, cousin, of the proclamation of universal peace and harmony among all kinds of beasts and birds? We are no longer to hunt and devour one another, but to love and help each other. Do come down, and we can talk over this great news at our leisure." The Cock, who knew that the Fox was only up to his old tricks, pretended to be watching something in the distance. The Fox asked him what it was he looked at so earnestly. "Why," said the Cock, "I think I see a pack of Hounds coming." "Oh, then," said the Fox, "I must go." "No, cousin," said the Cock; "please do not go: I am just coming down. You are surely not afraid of Dogs in these peaceful times!" "No, no," said the Fox; "but they may not have heard the proclamation yet."

MORAL: *Those who use deceit to get what they want are often caught in their own trap.*

The Hare and the Tortoise

One day, the Hare was laughing at the Tortoise for his slow and ungainly walk, so the Tortoise challenged him to a race. The Hare, looking on the whole affair as a great joke, agreed, and the Fox was selected to act as umpire and hold the stakes. The race began, and the Hare, of course, soon left the Tortoise far behind. When she reached midway to the finish line, she began to play and nibble the young grass and amuse herself in many ways. Because the day was so warm, she even thought she would take a little nap in a shady spot; even if the Tortoise should pass her while she slept, she could easily overtake him again before he reached the end. The Tortoise, however, plodded steadily on, unwavering and unresting, straight toward the finish line. Meanwhile, the Hare woke up suddenly from her nap, and was surprised to find that the Tortoise was nowhere in sight. Off she went at full speed, but when she got to the finish, she found that the Tortoise was already there, waiting for her arrival.

MORAL: Slow and steady wins the race.

Jupiter's Two Wallets

When Jupiter made Man, he gave him two Wallets—one for his neighbor's faults, the other for his own. He threw them over the Man's shoulder, so that one Wallet hung in front and the other behind. The Man kept the one in front for his neighbor's faults, and the one behind for his own. So, while the first was always under his nose, it took some effort to see the latter. This custom, which began so long ago, is still in practice today.

MORAL: Though people are often blind to their own faults, they rarely lose sight of their neighbor's.

The Stag Looking into the Pool

A Stag, drinking at a clear pool, admired the handsome look of his spreading antlers, but was very unhappy with the slim and ungainly appearance of his legs. "What a glorious pair of branching horns!" he said. "How gracefully they hang over my forehead! What an agreeable look they give my face! But as for my spindly legs, I am quite ashamed of them." The words were scarcely out of his mouth when he saw some huntsmen and a pack of hounds coming toward him. His despised legs soon placed him at a distance from his followers, but when he entered the forest, his horns got tangled at every turn and the dogs soon reached him. "Mistaken fool that I was!" he exclaimed; "had it not been for these wretched horns my legs would have saved my life."

MORAL: People often don't know their own strengths and weaknesses.

The Old Woman and the Doctor

An Old Woman with bad eyes called in a clever Doctor, who agreed to cure them for a certain price. He was a very clever Doctor, but he was also a very great rogue, and when he called each day and bandaged the Old Woman's eyes, he carried away with him some article of her furniture while she was blindfolded. This went on until he told the Woman she was cured. (By this time, her room was nearly bare.) When he claimed his fee, the Old Lady protested that, rather than being cured, her sight was worse than ever. "We will soon see about that, my good Woman," said the Doctor, and soon the old Woman was summoned to appear in Court. "May it please your Honor," she said to the Judge, "before I hired this Doctor, I could see many things in my room that now, when he says I am cured, I cannot see at all." The Court then realized what the Doctor had been up to, and he was forced to give the Old Woman her property back again, and was not allowed to claim a penny of his fee.

MORAL: Those who concentrate so intently on getting things dishonestly often don't see when they have provided evidence of their own misconduct.

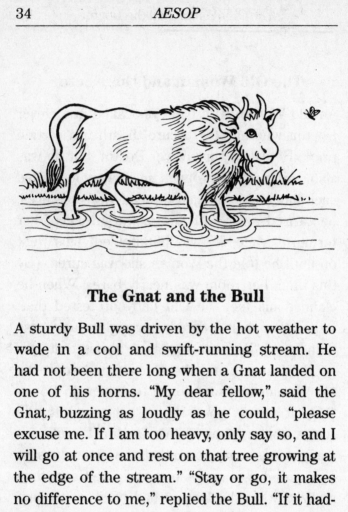

The Gnat and the Bull

A sturdy Bull was driven by the hot weather to wade in a cool and swift-running stream. He had not been there long when a Gnat landed on one of his horns. "My dear fellow," said the Gnat, buzzing as loudly as he could, "please excuse me. If I am too heavy, only say so, and I will go at once and rest on that tree growing at the edge of the stream." "Stay or go, it makes no difference to me," replied the Bull. "If it hadn't been for your buzz, I wouldn't even have known you were there."

MORAL: Some people are so weak that it doesn't make any difference whether they are there or not, since they cannot do either harm or good.

The Boy and the Figs

A Boy once thrust his hand into a jar full of figs and nuts. He grasped as many as his fist could possibly hold, but when he tried to take it out, the narrowness of the jar's neck prevented him. Not liking to lose any of them, but unable to take out his hand, he burst into tears and bitterly cried over his bad luck. An honest fellow who stood nearby gave him this wise and reasonable advice: "Grasp only half the quantity, my boy, and you will easily succeed."

MORAL: Greed often hinders success.

Socrates and His Friends

Socrates once built a house, and everybody who saw it had something bad to say about it. "What an ugly front!" said one. "What a poorly designed interior!" said another. "What rooms! not big enough to turn round in," said a third. "Small as it is," answered Socrates, "I wish I had true Friends enough to fill it."

MORAL: Though many people call themselves your friends, it is difficult to find loyal ones.

The Wolf and the Ass

The Wolves once selected one of their number as ruler. The Wolf that was chosen was a smooth-spoken rascal, and soon after he had been elected, he addressed an assembly of the Wolves as follows: "One thing," he said, "is so important and will ensure our general welfare so much, that I cannot stress it too much. Nothing promotes true brotherly feeling and the general good as much as the suppression of all selfishness. Let each one of you, then, share with any hungry brother who may be near whatever you catch while hunting." "Hear, hear!" cried an Ass, who had listened to the speech. "And of course you yourself will begin with the fat Sheep that you hid yesterday in a corner of your lair."

MORAL: Those who propose and enact just laws should live by them as well.

The Crow and the Pitcher

A Crow, about to die with thirst, flew with joy to a Pitcher, hoping to find some water in it. But all that was there was a little drop at the bottom, which he was quite unable to reach. First, he tried to break the Pitcher, but he was not strong enough. He then tried to overturn it, but it was too heavy. Finally, he gathered up some pebbles and, taking them one by one in his beak, dropped them into the Pitcher. In this way, the water gradually reached the top, and he was able to drink it easily.

MORAL: Necessity is the mother of invention.

The Mule Laden with Corn and the Mule Laden with Gold

Two Mules were being driven along a lonely road. One was loaded with Corn, and the other with Gold. The one that carried the Gold was so proud of his burden that, although it was very heavy, he would not for the world have the least bit of it taken away. He trotted along with a stately step, his bells jingling as he went. By-and-by, some Robbers caught them. They let the Mule that carried the Corn go free; but they took the Gold that the other carried, and because he kicked and struggled to prevent their robbing him, they stabbed him to the heart. Dying, he said to the other Mule, "I see, brother, it is not always a good thing to have grand duties to perform. If, like you, I had only carried Corn, I would be well now."

MORAL: The poor and humble live safely; the rich are always in danger.

The Fox and the Goat

A Fox had fallen into a well, and had been trying to get out for a long time. At length, a Goat came along, and wanting to drink, asked Reynard whether the water was good, and if there was plenty of it. The Fox, disguising the real danger of his case, replied, "Come down, my friend. The water is so good that I can't drink enough of it, and there's so much that the supply cannot be exhausted." Hearing this, the Goat without any more ado leaped in. The Fox, climbing over his friend's horns, then nimbly leaped out and coolly remarked to the poor deluded Goat: "If you had half as much brains as you have beard, you would have looked before you leaped."

MORAL: Look before you leap.

The Kid and the Wolf

A Kid, standing safely on a high rock, began to insult and jeer at a Wolf on the ground below. The Wolf, looking up, replied, "Do not think, vain creature, that you annoy me. I regard your insults as coming not from you, but from the place upon which you stand."

MORAL: It's easy to be brave when you're far from danger.

The Goose That Laid the Golden Egg

A certain man had the good fortune to possess a Goose that laid a Golden Egg every day. But unhappy with only one egg a day, he decided to kill the Goose and get the whole treasure at once. But, when he cut her open, he found her just like any other goose.

MORAL: Those who have much want more and so lose all.

Mercury and the Woodman

A Man felling a tree on the bank of a river, accidentally let his axe slip from his hand. It dropped into the water and sank to the bottom.

Greatly distressed at the loss of his tool, he sat down on the bank and grieved bitterly. Mercury appeared and asked him what was the matter. Having heard the Man's story, he dove to the bottom of the river, and bringing up a golden axe, offered it to him. The Woodman refused to take it, saying it was not his. Mercury then dove a second time, and brought up a silver one. The Man refused again, saying that that was not his either. Mercury dove a third time, and brought up the axe that the Man had lost, which he accepted with great joy and thankfulness. Mercury was so pleased with his honesty, that he gave him the other two axes as well. When the Woodman told this adventure to his friends, one of them set off for the river at once, and let his axe fall in on purpose. He then began to lament his loss with a loud voice. Mercury appeared as before, and demanded the cause of his grief. After hearing the Man's story, he dove and brought up a golden axe, and asked him if that was his. Overjoyed at the sight of the precious metal, the fellow eagerly answered that it was, and greedily tried to snatch it. The god, knowing that the Man lied, not only declined to give it to him, but refused to let him have his own again.

MORAL: Honesty is the best policy.

The Wolf and the Crane

A Wolf devoured his prey so ravenously that a bone stuck in his throat, causing him great pain. He ran howling up and down, and offered a handsome reward to anyone who would pull it out. A Crane, moved by pity as well as by the prospect of a reward, undertook the dangerous task. After removing the bone, he asked for the promised reward. "Reward!" jeered the Wolf; "you greedy fellow, what reward can you possibly require? You have had your head in a Wolf's mouth, and pulled it out unharmed. Get away and don't come again within reach of my paw."

MORAL: Those who are charitable in the hope of reward shouldn't be surprised if, in dealing with evil men, they receive more jeers than thanks.

The Boys and the Frogs

A group of Boys playing at the edge of a pond saw a number of Frogs in the water, and they began to throw stones at them. They had killed many of the poor creatures, when one braver than the rest put his head above the water and cried out to them: "Stop your cruel sport, my lads; remember, what is Play to you is Death to us."

MORAL: Things that seem unimportant to some are matters of great consequence to others.

The Hare and the Hound

A Dog, after chasing a Hare for a long time, finally ran out of breath and was forced to give up the pursuit. The owner of the Dog then teased him about letting the Hare outrun him. "Ah, master," answered the Dog, "it's all very well for you to laugh, but we were not running for the same reason. He was running for his life, while I was only running for my dinner."

MORAL: Survival is the greatest motivation to win the race.

The Ape and the Dolphin

A ship, wrecked off the coast of Greece, had a large Ape on board, kept for the amusement of the sailors. When the ship went down, the Ape, with most of the crew, was left struggling in the water. Some Dolphins, which are said to have a great friendship for man, were swimming nearby, and one of them, mistaking the Ape for a man, came to his rescue and swam with him to the mouth of the Piraeus (a harbor in Greece). "In what part of Greece do you live?" demanded the Dolphin. "I am an Athenian," said the Ape. "Oh, then, you know Piraeus, of course?" said the Dolphin, referring to the harbor. "Know Piraeus!" cried the Ape, not wishing to appear ignorant to the Dolphin. "I should think so. Why, my father and he are first cousins." Thereupon the Dolphin, finding that he had rescued an impostor, slipped from beneath his legs, and left him to his fate.

MORAL: *Those ignorant of the truth themselves often think they can deceive others with lies.*

The Goat and the Lion

The Lion, seeing a Goat playing and skipping up on a steep craggy rock, called to him to come down to the green pasture where he stood, and where he would be able to feed in much greater comfort. The Goat, who saw through the Lion's trick, replied, "Many thanks for your advice, dear Lion, but I wonder whether you are thinking most of my comfort, or of how much you would relish a nice morsel of Goat's flesh."

MORAL: *Those who use trickery and deceit shouldn't be surprised when it doesn't work.*

The Ploughman and Fortune

One day as a Countryman was ploughing his field, he came across a great store of treasure. Transported with joy, he fell upon the earth and thanked her for her kindness and liberality. Fortune appeared, and said to him, "You thank the ground warmly, and never think of me. If, instead of finding this treasure, you had lost it, I would have been the first one you blamed."

MORAL: It is easier to blame Fortune for our bad luck than to praise it for our good luck.

The Fox and the Ass

An Ass, finding a Lion's skin, put it on and stalked about the forest. The beasts fled in terror, and he was delighted at the success of his disguise. Meeting a Fox, he rushed at him, and this time he tried to imitate the roaring of the lion as well. "Ah!" said the Fox, "if you had held your tongue, I should have been deceived like the rest; but now that you bray, I know who you are."

MORAL: Those who assume a character that does not belong to them usually betray themselves by overacting it.

The Cats and the Mice

In times past, a fierce and lasting war raged between the Cats and Mice, in which the Mice always had to retreat. One day when the Mice were discussing the cause of their ill-luck, everyone agreed that it was because no one knew who their leaders were. So it was decided that in future each chief of a division should have his head decorated with distinctive ornaments, so that all the Mice would know where to look for orders. After the chiefs had drilled and disciplined their troops, they once more gave battle to the Cats. But the poor Mice again met with no better success. For while most of them reached their holes in safety, the chiefs were prevented from entering their retreats by their decorated headgear, and each of the chiefs were killed by their ruthless pursuers.

MORAL: There is no distinction without its accompanying risks.

The Peacock and the Crane

The Peacock, spreading his gorgeous tail, strutted up and down in his most stately manner before a Crane, and laughed at him for his plain feathers. "Tut, tut!" said the Crane; "which is better, to strut about in the dirt, and be gazed at by children, or to soar above the clouds, as I do?"

MORAL: Those who are most conceited often have the least cause.

The Man and the Lion

A Man and a Lion once argued together as to which belonged to the nobler race. The Man called the attention of the Lion to a statue of a Man strangling a Lion. "That proves nothing at all," said the Lion; "if a Lion had been the carver, he would have made the Lion conquering the Man."

MORAL: Consider the source of the evidence before believing it.

The Old Hound

An Old Hound, who had once been a great hunter, caught a Stag, but from feebleness and the loss of his teeth, he was forced to let it go. His master, therefore, began to beat the Old Dog cruelly, but stopped when the poor animal addressed him as follows: "Stop, dear master! You know well that I lack neither courage nor will, but only my strength and my teeth, and these I have lost in your service."

MORAL: Don't pass judgment until circumstances have been weighed.

The Two Travelers

As two Men were traveling through the woods, one of them picked up an axe that he saw lying on the ground. "Look here," he said to his companion, "I have found an axe." "Don't say '*I* have found it,'" said the other, "but '*We* have found it.' Since we are companions, we ought to share it." The first would not, however, consent. They had not gone far, when they heard the owner of the axe calling after them angrily. "We're in for it now!" said the Traveler who had the axe. "No," answered the other, "say '*I*'m in for it!'—not *we*. You wouldn't let me share the prize, so I'm not going to share the danger."

MORAL: If we're not willing to share good fortune with our friends, we shouldn't be surprised if they are unwilling to help in bad times.

The Ass and the Little Dog

An Ass observed how much his master loved his Little Dog, how much he caressed and fondled him, and fed him choice bits at every

meal—and for no other reason, that the Ass could see, but that he skipped and frisked about, wagging his tail. The ass, therefore, decided to imitate the Dog and see whether the same behavior would bring him similar favors. So one day, when the master had come home from walking and was seated in his easy chair, the Ass came into the room and danced around him with many an awkward step. The man could not help laughing aloud at the odd sight. The joke, however, became serious when the Ass, rising on his hindlegs, laid his forefeet on his master's shoulders and braying in his face, tried to jump into his lap. When the man cried out for help, one of his servants ran in with a stick and drove the poor Ass back to his stable, where he gladly stayed.

MORAL: Always be yourself and do not foolishly imitate others.

The Fox and the Grapes

One day a hungry Fox saw some tempting Grapes hanging high up from the ground. He made many attempts to reach them, but all in vain. Tired out by his failures, he walked off grumbling to himself, "They are sour, anyway, and not at all fit for eating."

MORAL: When people can't get what they want because of their own inabilities, they often pretend they didn't want it anyway.

The Fox in the Well

An unlucky Fox, after falling into a Well, could barely keep his head above water. As he was struggling, and sticking his claws into the side of the Well, a Wolf came by and looked in. "What! my dear brother," he said, with affected concern, "can it really be you that I see down there? How cold you must feel! How long have you been there? How did you fall in? I am so

sorry to see you in such trouble. Do tell me all about it!" "The end of a rope would be of more use to me than all your pity," answered the Fox. "Just help me get out of this well and you can have the whole story."

MORAL: There is a time for words and a time for action.

The Boy Who Cried Wolf

Once there was a mischievous Boy who used to watch over a flock of sheep near a village. As a joke, the Boy used to cry out, "Wolf! Wolf!" in order to see all the Villagers rush to his aid. When they discovered that there was no Wolf, the Boy just laughed at them. One day, after the

Boy had tricked the Villagers several times, a Wolf really did appear. But this time, when the Boy cried, "Wolf! Wolf!" the Villagers, who were tired of being laughed at, ignored his cries for help, and the whole flock was lost.

MORAL: If you tell a lot of lies, no one will believe you even when you tell the truth.

The Hart and the Vine

A Hart, who was being pursued by hunters, hid himself under the broad leaves of a shady, spreading Vine. When the hunters had gone by, he thought himself quite safe and began to eat the leaves of the Vine. The rustling of the branches drew the attention of the hunters, and they shot their arrows toward the sound and killed the Hart. As he lay dying, he admitted that he deserved his fate for ungratefully destroying the friend who had kindly sheltered him in time of danger.

MORAL: Ingratitude often leads to ruin.

The Sow and the Wolf

A Sow lay in the sty with her litter of newborn pigs all about her. A Wolf who longed to eat one of the piglets, but didn't know how to get one, tried to make friends with the mother in order to trick her. "How do you do today, Mrs. Sow?" she said. "A little fresh air would certainly do you great good. Now do go out for a walk, and I will gladly look after your young ones till you return." "Many thanks for your offer," replied the Sow. "But I know very well what kind of care you would take of my little ones. If you really wished to be as friendly as you pretend to be, you would not show me your face again."

MORAL: False words cannot disguise evil intent.

The Frog and the Ox

An Ox, grazing in a swampy meadow, accidentally set his foot among a brood of young Frogs, and crushed nearly all of them to death.

One that escaped ran off to his mother with the dreadful news. "And, O mother!" he said, "it was a beast—a big four-footed beast!—that did it." "Big?" asked the old Frog, "how big? Was it as big as this?" And she puffed herself out to a great degree. "Oh!" said the little one, "a great deal bigger than that." "Well, was it this big?" And she swelled herself out yet more. "Indeed, mother, it was; and if you were to burst yourself, you could never reach half its size." Provoked at such doubt of her powers, the old Frog made one more try, and really did burst herself.

MORAL: Some people are ruined by trying to be greater than they really are.

The Lion and the Mouse

A Lion, tired from hunting, lay sleeping under a shady tree. Some Mice scrambling over him while he slept, woke him. Laying his paw upon one of them, he was about to crush him, but the Mouse begged for mercy in such moving terms that he let him go. Some time after, the Lion was caught in a net laid by some hunters, and, unable to free himself, made the forest resound with his roars. The Mouse whose life had been spared came, and with his little sharp teeth soon gnawed through the ropes and set the Lion free.

MORAL: Kindness is seldom thrown away, and there is no creature so small that he cannot return a good deed.

The Stag and the Fawn

A Fawn once said to a Stag, "Why are you, who are so much bigger, and stronger, and faster than a Dog, so frightened when you see one? If you stood your ground and used your horns, I should think the Hounds would run from you." "I have said that to myself, little one, over and over again," replied the Stag, "and I've made up my mind to do it; but, no sooner do I hear a Dog than I am ready to jump out of my skin."

MORAL: If a man is born a coward, no amount of reasoning will make him a hero.

The Hen and the Fox

One night a Fox crept into a barn and looked up and down for something to eat. At last he spied a Hen, but she was sitting upon a perch so high that he could not reach her. He decided, then, to trick her. "Dear cousin," he said, speaking smoothly, "How do you do? I heard that you were ill, and stayed at home; I could not rest until I came to see you. Pray, let me feel your pulse. Indeed, you do not look well at all." He was running on in this impudent manner, when the Hen answered him from her roost, "Truly, dear Reynard, you are right. I have seldom been in more danger than I am now. Please excuse me for not coming down; but I am sure I should catch my death if I did." The Fox, realizing that the Hen was not deceived, made off, and tried his luck elsewhere.

MORAL: A deceitful nature cannot hide behind false kindness.

The Farmer and the Eagle

A Farmer, who was out walking one fine day, found an Eagle caught in a snare. Struck with the beauty of the bird, and being a kindhearted fellow, he let the Eagle go. The sun was shining fiercely, and the Man soon sought out a cool spot in the shadow of an old wall, where he sat down upon a stone. A few moments later, he was surprised by the Eagle swooping down upon his head and carrying off his hat. The bird flew off some distance, and then let it fall. The Man ran after his hat and picked it up, wondering why an Eagle to which he had shown so much kindness should play such a mischievous trick in return. As he turned round to go back to his seat by the wall, he was astonished to see, where the wall had just been, nothing but a heap of stones.

MORAL: An act of kindness is never wasted.

The Dove and the Ant

An Ant going to a river to drink, fell in and was carried along in the stream. A Dove pitied her condition, and threw a stick into the river, which helped the Ant get to shore. Soon afterwards, the Ant saw a man with a gun aiming at the Dove. Just as he was about to fire, the Ant stung him in the foot and made him miss his aim, so saving the Dove's life.

MORAL: One good turn deserves another.

The Mischievous Dog

A certain Man had a Dog that bothered so many people that he tied a heavy bell around his neck to warn people when he was near. The Dog, however, thought that the bell was a mark of honorable distinction, and grew so vain that he turned up his nose at all the other dogs. But a clever old Dog soon let him know that far from being a mark of honor, the bell was really a sign of disgrace.

MORAL: People often mistake notoriety for fame, and would rather be noticed for their faults than not noticed at all.

The Ass Laden with Salt and with Sponges

A Man drove his Ass to the seaside to purchase a load of Salt. On the way home, the Ass stumbled and fell while crossing a stream. It was some time before he was able to get back on his feet, and by that time, all the Salt had melted away. The Ass, however, was delighted to find that he had lost his burden. Some time later, the Ass was loaded with Sponges, and he came to the same stream. Remembering what had happened before, he stumbled this time on purpose, and was surprised to find that his load, instead of disappearing, had become even heavier than before.

MORAL: Being too clever can lead to disaster.

The Goatherd and the Goats

During a snowstorm one winter, a Goatherd drove his Goats for shelter to a large cavern where some Wild Goats had already taken refuge. The Man was so struck by the size and look of these Goats, and with their superior beauty to his own, that he gave them all the food he could collect and none to his own. The storm lasted many days, and the Tame Goats eventually died of starvation. As soon as the sun shone again, the strangers ran off to return to their native wilds. The Goatherd had to go goatless home, and was laughed at by everyone for his folly.

MORAL: If you neglect old friends for the sake of new ones, you might lose both.

The Farmer and His Sons

A certain Farmer, lying at the point of death, called his Sons around him and gave them all his fields and vineyards, telling them that a treasure lay hidden somewhere in them, within a foot from the ground. His Sons thought he was talking about money that he had buried, and after he died, they dug most industriously all over the farm, but found nothing. The soil was so well loosened, however, that the next crops were so rich that the Sons prospered. They then realized why their Father had told them to dig for hidden treasure.

MORAL: Hard work is a treasure in itself.

The Horse and the Lion

A Lion, who had become old and infirm, saw a fine plump Horse, and longed for a bit of him to eat. Knowing that the animal would prove too fast for him in the chase, he decided to outwit him. He told all the beasts that, having spent

many years studying medicine, he was now prepared to heal any illness they might have. (He
hoped by this means to get near them, and so
find a chance of satisfying his appetite.) The
Horse, who doubted the Lion's honesty, came
up limping, pretending that he had a thorn in
one of his hind feet, which gave him great pain.
The Lion asked to see his foot, and pored over
it with a mock earnest air. The Horse, slyly
looking around, saw that the Lion was about to
spring, and suddenly sending out both his heels
at once, gave him such a kick in the face, that it
laid him stunned and sprawling on the ground.
Then, laughing at the success of his trick, he
trotted merrily away.

MORAL: *If you try to gain by deceit, you
may also lose by it.*

The Ass, the Lion and the Cock

One day, an Ass and a Cock feeding in the same meadow were surprised by a Lion. The Cock crowed loudly, and the Lion (who is said to have a great hatred of the crowing of a Cock) at once turned tail and ran off. The Ass, believing that the Lion was afraid of him, pursued him. As soon as they could no longer hear the Cock's crow, however, the Lion turned round upon the Ass and tore him to pieces.

MORAL: Presumption begins in ignorance and ends in ruin.

The Lion, the Tiger and the Fox

A Lion and a Tiger happened to come together over the dead body of a Fawn that had been recently shot. A fierce battle began, and because each animal was in the prime of his age and strength, the fight was long and furious. At last they lay stretched on the ground panting, bleeding and exhausted, each unable to lift a paw against the other. An impudent Fox came by at this time, stepped in and carried off the Fawn right before their eyes.

MORAL: It is often better to share with the enemy than to lose everything in the fight.

The Fortune-Teller

A Man who claimed to be a Wizard and Fortune-teller, used to stand in the marketplace and pretend to tell fortunes, give information about missing property and other similar things. One day, while he was busily going about this business, a mischievous fellow broke through the crowd, and gasping as if he were out of breath, told him that his house was on fire and would shortly burn to the ground. At the news, the Wizard ran off as fast as his legs could carry him, while the Joker and a crowd of other people followed at his heels. But the house, it seems, was not on fire at all, and the Joker then asked him, amid the jeers of the people, how could he, who was so clever at telling other people's fortunes, know so little of his own?

MORAL: Those who practice deception are often most easily deceived.

The Oak and the Reeds

A violent storm uprooted an Oak that grew on the bank of a river. The Oak drifted across the stream, and lodged among some Reeds. Amazed that they were still standing, he could not help asking them how they had escaped the fury of a storm that had torn him up by the roots. "We bent our heads to the blast," they said, "and it passed over us. You stood stiff and stubborn till you could stand no longer."

MORAL: *Sometimes it is better to bend with forces that are too strong to oppose.*

The Fox and the Mask

A Fox was rummaging in the house of an actor one day, and came across a very beautiful Mask. Putting his paw on the forehead, he said, "What a handsome face we have here! What a pity that it should lack brains."

MORAL: A fair outside is a poor substitute for inner worth.

The Sick Lion

An old Lion, no longer able to hunt for his prey, laid himself up in his den and, breathing with great difficulty and speaking with a low voice, pretended that he was very ill. The report soon spread among the beasts, and there was great mourning for the sick Lion. One animal after the other came to see him; but, visiting him alone and in his own den, the Lion easily captured them, and soon grew fat. The Fox, suspecting the truth of the matter, eventually came to make his visit, and standing at some dis-

`tance, asked his Majesty how he did? "Ah, my dearest friend," said the Lion, "is it you? Why do you stand so far from me? Come, sweet friend, and pour a word of consolation in the poor Lion's ear, who has but a short time to live." "Bless you!" said the Fox, "but excuse me if I cannot stay; for, to tell the truth, I feel quite uneasy at the footprints that I see here, all pointing toward your den, and none returning outwards."

MORAL: It is easier to get into a bad situation than to get out of it; make sure there is a way out before you venture in.

Hercules and the Wagoner

As a Wagoner was driving his heavy wagon through a miry lane, the wheels stuck fast in the mud, and the Horses could go no further. The Man dropped on his knees and began crying and praying to Hercules to come and help him. "Lazy fellow!" said Hercules, "get up and stir yourself. Whip your Horses stoutly, and put your shoulder to the wheel. Then if you still need my help, you shall have it."

MORAL: If you want help from others, you must be willing to help yourself.

The Travelers and the Bear

Two men about to journey through a forest, agreed to stand by one another in any dangers that might arise. They had not gone far before a savage Bear rushed out from a thicket and stood in their path. One of the Travelers quickly scurried up into a tree. The other fell flat on his face and held his breath. The Bear came up and smelled him, and taking him for dead, went off again into the woods. The man in the tree came down, and rejoining his companion, asked him, with a mischievous smile, what was the wonderful secret that the Bear had whispered into his ear. "Why," the other sulkily replied, "he told me to be careful in the future and not to trust such cowardly rascals as you."

MORAL: *True friends stand together in bad times as well as good.*

The Falconer and the Partridge

A Partridge, captured in the net of a Falconer, begged the Man to set him free, and promised if he were let go, that he would decoy other Partridges into the net. "No," replied the Falconer; "I did not mean to let you go; but if I had, your words would now have condemned you. The scoundrel who tries to save himself by betraying his friends deserves worse than death."

MORAL: *Those who are willing to betray their friends to save themselves may lose their honor as well as their lives.*

The Wind and the Sun

A dispute once arose between the North Wind and the Sun as to which was the stronger of the two. Seeing a traveler on his way, they agreed that whichever could make him take off his cloak first was the strongest. The North Wind began, and sent a furious blast, which nearly tore the cloak from its fastenings; but the traveler, seizing the garment with a firm grip, held it round his body so tightly that the Wind failed in his efforts. The Sun, scattering the clouds that had gathered, then darted his warmest beams on the traveler's head. Growing faint with the heat, the man flung off his cloak, and ran for protection to the nearest shade.

MORAL: Persuasion is better than force, and a kind and gentle manner will get quicker results than threats.

The Lion, the Fox and the Ass

An Ass and a Fox had made an alliance, and were rambling through a forest one day when they were met by a Lion. The Fox was seized with great fear and taking the first opportunity of speaking with the Lion, he tried to ensure his own safety at the expense of the Ass. "Sire," he said, "this Ass is young and plump, and if your majesty would care to make a dinner of him, I know how he might be caught without much trouble. There is a pit not far away, into which I can easily lead him." The Lion agreed, and after the Ass had been caught, he began his dinner by devouring the traitorous Fox, saving the Ass to be eaten later.

MORAL: Those who betray their friends often find themselves destroyed as well.

The Fox and the Crow

A Crow, after stealing a piece of cheese from a cottage window, flew with it to a tree that was some way off. A Fox, drawn by the smell of the cheese, came and sat at the foot of the tree, and tried to find some way to get it. "Good morning, dear Miss Crow," said he. "How well you are looking today! What handsome feathers you have, to be sure! Perhaps, too, your voice is as sweet as your feathers are fine. If so, you are really the Queen of Birds." The Crow, quite beside herself to hear such praise, at once opened her beak wide to let the Fox hear her voice, dropping the cheese as she did. The Fox snapped it up, and exclaimed, "Ah! ah! my dear Miss Crow, you must learn that all who flatter have their own ends in view. And that lesson will well repay you for a bit of cheese."

MORAL: Those who listen to false flatterers must pay the price.

The Wanton Calf

A Calf, full of play and wantonness, saw an Ox pulling a plough, and could not help insulting him. "What a sorry poor drudge are you," he said, "to bear that heavy yoke on your neck, and with a plough at your tail all day, to go turning up the ground for a master. You are a wretched poor slave, and know no better, or you wouldn't do it.

See what a happy life I lead; I go just where I please—sometimes in the cool shade, sometimes in the warm sunshine; and whenever I like I drink at the clear running brook." The Ox, not at all bothered by these insults, went on quietly and calmly with his work. That evening, unyoked and going to take his rest, he saw the Calf, decorated with garlands of flowers, being led off for sacrifice by the priests. He pitied him, but could not help asking him, "Now, friend, whose condition is better, yours or mine?"

MORAL: It is better to work hard and live long than to sacrifice your life for fleeting pleasures.

The Old Man and His Sons

An Old Man had many Sons who were always quarrelling with one another. He had often begged them to live together in harmony, but without success. One day he called them together, and producing a bundle of sticks, he asked them each to try and break it. Each tried with all his strength, but the bundle resisted their efforts. Then, cutting the cord that bound the sticks together, the Old Man told his Sons to break them separately. This was done with the greatest ease. "See, my Sons," he exclaimed, "the power of unity! Bound together by brotherly love, you can defy almost every mortal ill; divided, you will fall a prey to your enemies."

MORAL: *In unity there is strength.*

The Satyr and the Traveler

A Satyr, walking in the forest one winter, came across a Traveler half starved with the cold. He took pity on him and invited him to his cave. On their way the Man kept blowing on his fingers. "Why do you do that?" asked the Satyr, who had seen little of the world. "To warm my hands. They are nearly frozen," replied the Man. At the cave, the Satyr poured out some steaming porridge and set it before the Traveler, who immediately began blowing on it with all his might. "What, blowing again?" cried the Satyr. "Is it not hot enough?" "Yes," answered the Man, "it is too hot, and that is why I am blowing on it." "Be off with you!" said the Satyr, in alarm. "I will have nothing to do with a man who can blow hot and cold from the same mouth."

MORAL: *Constancy is a good measure of trustworthiness.*

The Maid and the Pail of Milk

A Country Milkmaid was on her way to market, to sell a pail of new Milk, which she carried on her head. As she was tripping gaily along, she thought, "For this Milk I shall get a shilling, and with that shilling I shall buy twenty of the eggs laid by our neighbor's fine hens. If only half of the chicks from these eggs grow up and thrive before the next fair comes around, I can sell them for a good price. Then I shall buy that jacket I saw in the village the other day, and a hat and ribbons too, and when I go to the fair how pretty I will look! Robin will be there, for certain, and he will come up and offer to be friends again. I won't come round so easily, though; and when he tries to kiss me, I shall just toss my head and—" Here the Maid gave her head the toss she was thinking about. Down came the Pail, and the Milk ran out on the ground! And all her imaginary plans came to nothing.

MORAL: Don't count your chickens until they're hatched.

The Frogs Asking for a King

A long, long time ago, when the Frogs were all at liberty in the lakes, and had grown quite weary of their complete freedom, they assembled one day together to petition Jupiter to let them have a King to keep them in better order and make them lead more honest lives. Jupiter, knowing the vanity of their hearts, smiled at their request, and threw down a Log into the lake. The splash and commotion it made sent the whole assembly into the greatest terror and amazement. They rushed under the water and into the mud, and dared not come near the spot where it lay. At length one Frog bolder than the rest ventured to pop his head above the water and take a look at their new King from a respectful distance. Presently, when the Frogs saw the Log remain stock-still, others began to swim up to it and around it; soon, growing bolder and bolder, they at last leaped on it, and treated it with the greatest contempt. Dissatisfied with so tame a ruler, they petitioned Jupiter a second time for another, more active King. At this request, he sent them a Stork, who no sooner arrived among them than he began devouring them one by one as fast as he could. Then they sent Mercury with a private

message to Jupiter, begging him to take pity on them once more. But Jupiter replied that they were only suffering the punishment they deserved for their folly, and that the next time, they would learn to let well enough alone, and not be dissatisfied with their natural condition.

MORAL: It is better to have a harmless ruler than a cruel tyrant.

The Farmer and the Stork

A Farmer set a net in his fields to catch the Cranes and Geese that came to eat his new corn. He caught several, and with them a Stork, who pleaded for his life on the ground that he was neither a Goose nor a Crane, but a poor harmless Stork. "That may be very true," replied the Farmer. "But since I have caught you in bad company, you must expect to suffer the same punishment."

MORAL: People are often judged by the company they keep.

The Dog in the Manger

A Dog was lying in a manger full of hay, when a hungry Ox came near to eat. But the Dog, getting up and snarling at him, wouldn't let the Ox have any of the hay. "Surly creature," said the Ox, "You can't eat the hay yourself, but you still won't let anyone else have it."

MORAL: Some people are so selfish they won't share even the things which they cannot use.

The Boasting Traveler

One day a Man was entertaining a crowd with an account of the wonders he had done when abroad on his travels. "I was once at Rhodes," he said, "and the people of Rhodes, you know, are famous for jumping. Well, I took a jump there that no other man could come within a yard of. That's a fact, and if we were there I could bring you ten men who would prove it." "What need is there to go to Rhodes for witnesses?" asked one of his hearers. "Just imagine that you are there now, and show us your leap."

MORAL: Don't boast about something unless you're ready to prove it with actions.